Received On

DEC 0 8 2020

Magnolia Library

NO LONGER PROPERTY OF
~~~~~~~~~~~~~~~~~~ LIBRARY

D0819940

One EARTH

ISBN: 978-1-5460-1539-0

WorthyKids
Hachette Book Group
1290 Avenue of the Americas
New York, NY 10104

Text copyright © 2020 by Eileen Spinelli
Art copyright © 2020 by Hachette Book Group, Inc.

All rights reserved. No part of this publication may be reproduced or transmitted in any form or by any means, electronic or mechanical, including photocopy, recording, or any information storage and retrieval system, without permission in writing from the publisher.

WorthyKids is a registered trademark of Hachette Book Group, Inc.

Library of Congress Cataloging-in-Publication Data

Names: Spinelli, Eileen, author. | Coelho, Rogério, illustrator.
Title: One earth / written by Eileen Spinelli ; illustrated by Rogério
 Coelho.
Description: Hardcover. | New York : WorthyKids, 2020. | Audience: Ages
 4–8. | Summary: An illustrated counting rhyme that celebrates the beauty
 of nature and recommends ways to protect our one and only world,
 including recycling, conserving energy, and repairing broken items.
Identifiers: LCCN 2019052196 | ISBN 9781546015390 (hardcover)
Subjects: CYAC: Stories in rhyme. | Nature—Fiction. | Conservation of
 natural resources—Fiction. | Counting.
Classification: LCC PZ8.3.S759 One 2020 | DDC [E]—dc23
LC record available at https://lccn.loc.gov/2019052196

Designed by Eve DeGrie

Printed and bound in Canada
FRI
10 9 8 7 6 5 4 3 2 1

The mark of responsible forestry

One EARTH

Written by **Eileen Spinelli**

Illustrated by
Rogério Coelho

WORTHY
kids

One wide, sweeping sky.
Two honeybees.

Three bunnies in a nest.
Four redwood trees.

Five clumps of yellow flowers.
Six turtles snoozing.

Seven dolphins in the sea.
Eight seagulls cruising.

Nine worms underground.
Ten fields to plow.

Celebrating
Earth—

counting backwards now.

Ten scraps of litter?
  Toss them in the trash.
Nine empty bottles?
  Turn them in for cash.

Eight plastic grocery bags?
Weave them into mats.
Seven towels getting thin?
Good for shelter cats.

Six flannel shirts—too old?
Cozier than new.
Five lamps to light a room?
Try to use just two.

Four pairs of socks with holes?
You can learn to sew.

Three avocado seeds?
Plant and watch
them grow.

Two broken bicycles?
Fixing can be fun.

Almost finished counting
now—we're down to one.

One moon.

One sun.
One Earth
so beautiful.

Remember—
only one.